Dear Parent:
Your child's love of reac...

Every child learns to read in a different way and at his or her own speed. Some go back and forth between reading levels and read favorite books again and again. Others read through each level in order. You can help your young reader improve and become more confident by encouraging his or her own interests and abilities. From books your child reads with you to the first books he or she reads alone, there are I Can Read Books for every stage of reading:

SHARED READING
Basic language, word repetition, and whimsical illustrations, ideal for sharing with your emergent reader

BEGINNING READING
Short sentences, familiar words, and simple concepts for children eager to read on their own

READING WITH HELP
Engaging stories, longer sentences, and language play for developing readers

READING ALONE
Complex plots, challenging vocabulary, and high-interest topics for the independent reader

ADVANCED READING
Short paragraphs, chapters, and exciting themes for the perfect bridge to chapter books

I Can Read Books have introduced children to the joy of reading since 1957. Featuring award-winning authors and illustrators and a fabulous cast of beloved characters, I Can Read Books set the standard for beginning readers.

A lifetime of discovery begins with the magical words **"I Can Read!"**

Visit www.icanread.com for information on enriching your child's reading experience.

To Luke
—K.G.

To my daughter,
who loves to make bubbles
in the bath
—O.V.

Typography by Joe Merkel

Library of Congress Control Number: 2015956254
ISBN 978-0-06-235312-2 (hardcover) — ISBN 978-0-06-235311-5 (pbk.)

20 21 22 CWM 15 ❖ First Edition

I Can Read! My First SHARED READING

DUCK, DUCK, DINOSAUR

BUBBLE BLAST

Written by Kallie George

Illustrated by Oriol Vidal

HARPER
An Imprint of HarperCollins*Publishers*

This is Feather.

This is Flap.

And this is their brother, Spike.

It is summer.

Time for fun.

Big fun.

Small fun.

Summer fun!

Feather, Flap, and Spike get dirty.

Very dirty.

"Time for a bath," says Mama.

“No,” says Feather.

“Baths are not fun.”

“No bath. No bath,” says Flap.

"BATH!" says Spike.

Spike jumps into the pond.

Feather and Flap do not.

“Time for soap,” says Mama.

"No," says Feather. "Soap is not fun."

"No soap. No soap," says Flap.

"SOAP!" says Spike.

Spike takes a bar of soap.

Feather and Flap do not.

"Time for scrubbing," says Mama.

“No,” says Feather. “Scrubbing is not fun.”

“No scrubbing. No scrubbing,” says Flap.

“SCRUB!” says Spike.

Spike scrubs with a sponge.

Feather and Flap do not.

"Feather and Flap!" says Mama.

"It is time for soap.

It is time to scrub.

It is time for . . ."

"Bubbles?" asks Spike.

“Yes!” says Feather. “Bubbles are fun!”

“Yes bubbles! Yes bubbles!” says Flap.

"BUBBLES!" says Spike.

Feather and Flap jump into the pond.

Soon, bubbles are everywhere.

Big bubbles.

Small bubbles.

Bubbles are fun.

And bath time is fun, too!

DANGER BEASTS

ENTER AT YOUR OWN RISK

CONTENTS

Editor: Paddy Kempshall
Senior Art Editor: Daniel Rachael
Sub-Editor: Siobhan Keeler

Introduction:
Tim Haines and Jasper James
Scientific advice: Dr Paul Chambers
Series advice: Josie Sekulin

Printed and bound in Belgium by Proost NV.
Colour origination by Polestar Imaging, Watford Ltd.
ISBN 0 563 53311 0

WORKING WITH BEASTS

Introduction by Jasper James, Series Producer and Tim Haines, Executive Producer, *Walking with Beasts.*

Since *Walking with Dinosaurs,* Jasper James and Tim Haines have been busy bringing some more amazing creatures to life. Here's what they had to say about the making of this new series:

"*Walking with Beasts* took us two and a half years to make, with over 60 people involved and at least 400 scientists consulted. We're going to open the lid on a whole hidden period of pre-history – this is showing people stuff they didn't know they didn't know about!"

What are your favourite/least favourite beasts?
Jasper: I've got a soft spot for the Indricotheres – gentle giants that they are. I'm also in awe of *Gastornis* – they're vicious giants. The beast I'd least like to have as a pet is Entelodont – it's a disgusting combination of bad breath and bad attitude.
Tim: My favourites are the Terror Birds (*Gastornis* and *Phorusrhacos*) and my least favourite has to be Entelodont – it's so ugly!

What does the future hold?
Jasper: We now have the technology to bring to life anything that doesn't or has never existed. Other than that, we're not telling, but be prepared for a big surprise!

What was the funniest moment?
Jasper: When we filmed a woolly rhino charging the *Neanderthal*. The rhino head was mounted on a battering ram and then everyone ran as fast they could towards this poor actor!

...And the scariest?
Jasper: When we were crossing a rough patch of sea to get to a location, a big wave put the entire boat underwater for a few seconds. I'm sure it felt worse than it was. The captain didn't look too worried though – then again, he wasn't feeling well anyway!

Gastornis

Entelodont

Did the crew play tricks on each other?
Jasper: Give a group of people a bunch of hairy rubber animals and tricks are bound to happen...

If you could make up your own beast, what would it be?
Jasper: A woolly whale.
Tim: A sabre-tooth human.

How did you make the blood and how much was used?
Jasper: It was a sugar syrup mixed with red dye and we used gallons of it. The wasps really loved it!

"...be prepared for a big surprise!"

Entelodont

Smilodon

What was the most expensive element of the series?
Jasper: Possibly the actors in the Ice Age episode. You have to pay them, make their faces up, clothe them and put them up in hotels. The moving puppets just sit in a box until they're needed!
Tim: Solving the hair problem on the computer beasts. And *Mammoth* carcasses don't come cheap!

What other beasts did you think of using that never made it to the final cut?
Jasper: The Megatooth Shark of 3 million years ago – it was 15 times the size of a Great White. I'd love to have done this beast, but all the other creatures we feature at that time lived on land, so it didn't fit our story.
Tim: I was tempted by running crocodiles and giant kangaroos!

Where did you go to film the backgrounds?
Tim: Episode 1 was Java, Episode 2 – Florida and Mexico, Episode 3 – Utah, Episode 4 – South Africa, Episode 5 – Brazil, and Episode 6 – Canada.

Which do you think would win in a scrap – *T-rex* or *Megatherium*?
Tim: Even though the *Megatherium* has strong arms and huge claws, I think if *T-rex* was hungry and determined enough, it'd win in the end.
Jasper: I'm not one to condone animal fights, but if I were I'd be more interested to see *Smilodon* battle with *Utahraptor*. That'd be fast and furious and we'd see huge teeth versus huge claws. I think that *Smilodon* would come out on top because *Utahraptor* has a long vulnerable neck.

Thanks for answering our questions and giving us an inside look at what it's like working with beasts!

Utahraptor

KING OF THE DEEP

Here's a close-up of *Basilosaurus* – a monster marine muncher who's related to the whale:

This massive beast didn't only feed on other sea creatures. It was just as happy hunting land animals like this *Moeritherium*, just like a Killer Whale does today.

Unlike a modern whale, *Basilosaurus* probably used sight rather than sound to search for food.

At 18 metres long, *Basilosaurus* was the largest sea hunter of the time, easily dwarfing its close relative, *Dorudon*.

BASILOSAURUS (BASS-il-oh-SAWR-uss)

FULL NAME: *Basilosaurus isis*

MEANS: 'King lizard'

WHEN: 40 – 36 million years ago

WHERE: Fossils have been found in Louisiana, USA as well as in Egypt

SIZE: Up to 18 metres long – as long as a train carriage!

THE WORLD OF BEASTS

The prehistoric world was full of some of the strangest beasts ever to roam the planet. Here's a look at where some of these amazing creatures could be found:

MOERITHERIUM:

36 – 33 million years ago

Looking like a cross between a hippo and an elephant, remains of *Moeritherium* have been found at the Fayum deposits in Egypt, as well as other places in North and West Africa.

PHORUSRHACOS:

27 million – 15,000 years ago

Remains of this meat eating 'Terror Bird' have been found in Argentina as well as Texas and Florida. Once the top hunter, they were pushed aside by *Smilodon*.

MEGALOCEROS:

400,000 – 9,500 years ago

Megaloceros was found all over Europe. People used to think that they died out because their horns were too heavy for their heads!

DORUDON:

40 – 36 million years ago

Remains of this ocean beast have been found in Louisiana and Fayum, Egypt. It is so closely related to *Basilosaurus* that when the first fossil was found, it was mistaken for a baby *Basilosaurus*.

AMBULOCETUS:

50 – 49 million years ago

This early ancestor to the whales lived in the estuaries of prehistoric Pakistan. It lay in wait to drag its prey into the water and drown them.

prey: an animal hunted as food by another animal
estuary: the part of a river where it meets the sea

MAMMOTH MISSION

Can you find the hidden beasts?
Check out the list opposite and tick off the beasts when you've found them.

Mammoth

L	E	P	T	I	C
A	U	H	T	N	O
N	E	O	G	C	B
C	A	R	E	K	A
Y	O	U	S	H	S
L	A	S	T	A	T
O	T	R	H	T	O
T	U	H	R	T	A
H	Q	A	O	A	L
E	L	C	I	O	K
R	A	O	S	A	R
I	C	S	A	O	T
U	N	C	T	L	O
M	E	S	A	J	R
A	A	D	O	E	D
G	A	S	A	T	A
A	M	B	U	L	O

Time yourself and check your score here. Turn to page 56 to check the answers.

Less than 10 minutes: A mammoth achievement!

More than 10 minutes: A prehistoric effort!

Just how do you say all those long names? Here's our guide on how to pronounce them.

T	I	D	I	U	M
D	O	L	I	M	S
A	S	X	U	E	U
V	A	I	A	G	C
A	R	A	A	A	E
E	A	I	N	T	H
M	M	A	M	H	T
S	L	S	A	E	I
A	I	Y	N	R	P
N	U	A	C	I	O
S	A	P	A	U	L
O	L	Y	C	M	A
T	H	E	R	I	R
A	G	T	B	A	T
I	C	U	R	U	S
P	L	J	K	E	U
C	E	T	U	S	A

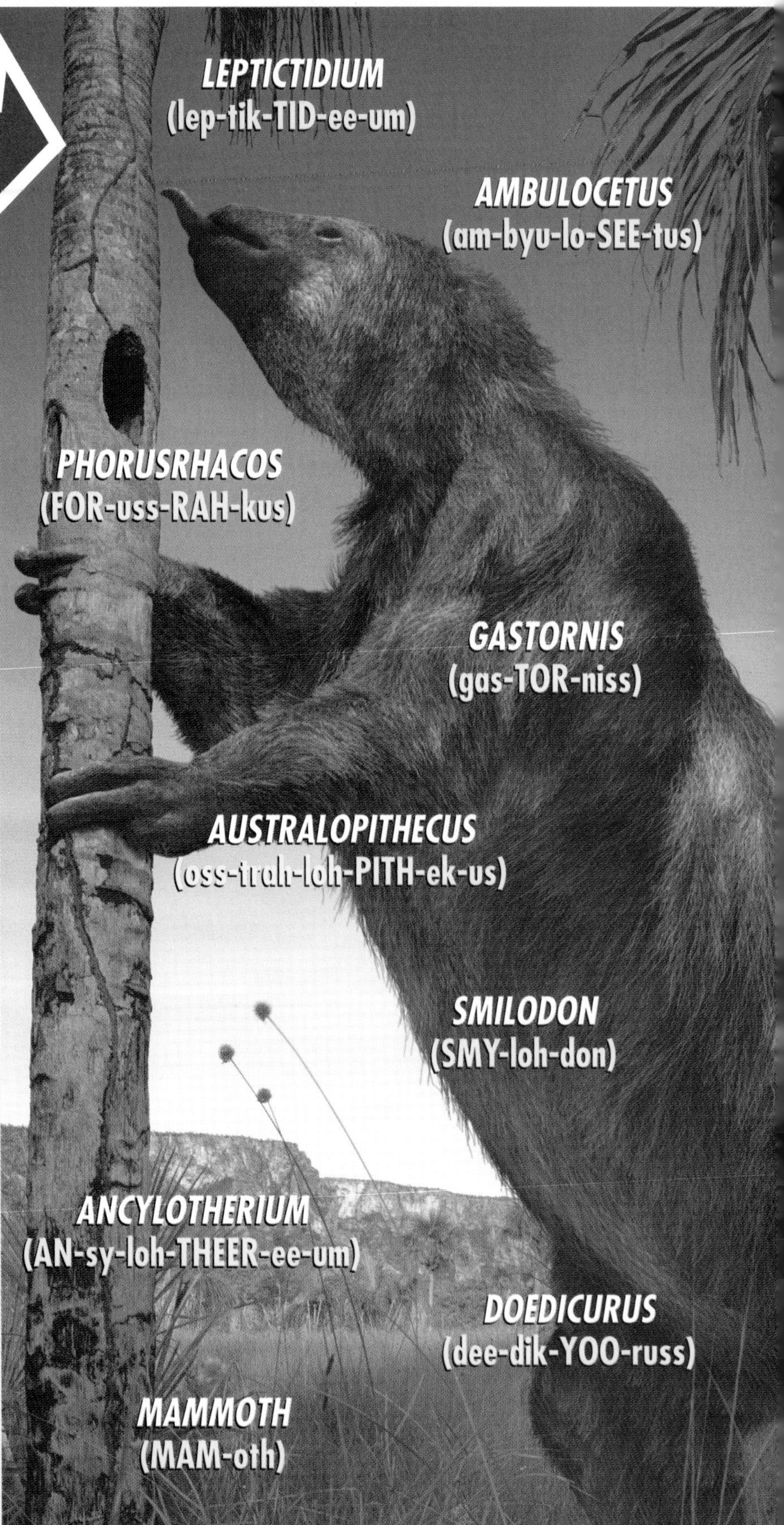

LEPTICTIDIUM
(lep-tik-TID-ee-um)

AMBULOCETUS
(am-byu-lo-SEE-tus)

PHORUSRHACOS
(FOR-uss-RAH-kus)

GASTORNIS
(gas-TOR-niss)

AUSTRALOPITHECUS
(oss-trah-loh-PITH-ek-us)

SMILODON
(SMY-loh-don)

ANCYLOTHERIUM
(AN-sy-loh-THEER-ee-um)

DOEDICURUS
(dee-dik-YOO-russ)

MAMMOTH
(MAM-oth)

MEGATHERIUM
(meg-ah-THEER-ee-um)

Megatherium

THE STORY OF THE

Part 1: Kazakstan; 50 million years ago

A survivor of the disaster that wiped out the dinosaurs, *Leptictidium* is a common sight.

One of the smallest mammals of the time, it lives its life at a hectic pace among the trees of tropical forests.

Every day is a drama of life and death – whether hunting for the large amounts of insects it needs to eat every day...

...or trying to avoid being a meal for something else!

BEASTS

Part 2: Pakistan; 35 million years ago

The natural successors to the great dinosaur plant-eaters, Brontotheres roam the land in herds.

Their huge size means that they have no natural land predators. But they are never truly safe from the attentions of other large beasts.

Indeed, with the changing climate and shifting land, a new predator has emerged – and this time it has come from the depths of the sea...

predator: an animal that kills and eats other animals

DATA BANK 1

GODINOTIA

(god-in-OH-sha)

- SIZE: Only 30cm long, with a long tail
- LIVED: 49 million years ago
- DIET: Mainly insects, but also fruit
- DID YOU KNOW: *Godinotia* only came out at night

It was a primate – that means it is a distant ancestor of humans!

MONSTER MUDDLE

We've mixed up two beasts. Can you work out which ones?

Unscramble the words to reveal the beasts.
The pictures might give you a clue.

i t d i u m L e i p c t

u d r D n o o

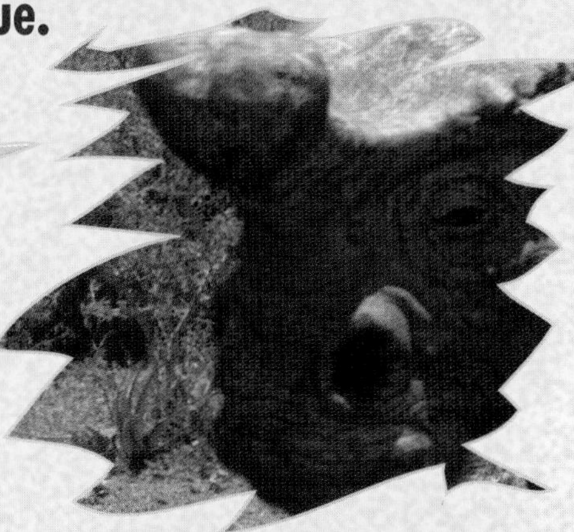

e r n t o B r o t h e

Answers:

The two beasts in the picture are *Chalicothere* and *Doedicurus*. The mixed-up words spell out *Leptictidium*, *Dorudon* and Brontothere.

FACE

Not all the beasts you see in the programme were completely created in a computer. The team also put together some special 'animatronic' puppets – just right for those extreme close-ups!

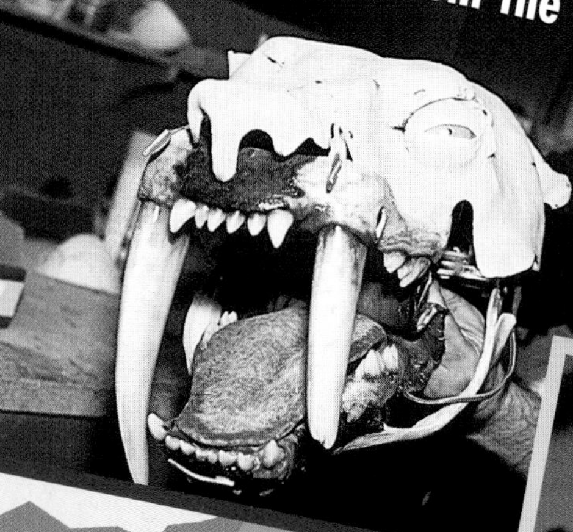

1) First of all a set of moulds are made from a clay model. Then a plastic head is made from the moulds.

2) Motors are added to help make the eyes open and close and other body parts move.

3) Mounts are also created to allow people to hold and operate the puppets. In some cases – like the full-size *Mammoth* that was made – it takes up to seven people to work one puppet!

4) Then the heads are painted and decorated with a special 'plastic' paint which doesn't crack when the puppet moves.

5

Fold is here

6

Fold is here

7

Fold is here

8

Fold is here

9

Fold is here

10

Fold is here

Illustrated by David Benham.

E) Then on the page in front of that, stick your next drawing in the centre and keep doing this until you've stuck in all 10 pictures.

F) Now flick your book from the back to the front and watch how *Doedicurus* comes lumbering out of the page!

lumbering: moving awkwardly/heavily

WALKING WITH

Just how big were these prehistoric beasts? Here's a chance to compare how you'd measure up to these mighty creatures...

Thanks to Miles. Child photography by Christopher Baines.

THE BEASTS
Part 1
g
h
i

The age of the beasts was a very dangerous time – an attack by a fierce predator was often only a step away. We just managed to catch Hyaenodon in action, and saw how quickly things can change...
STEP BY STEP
A group of Chalicothere are quietly grazing by the side of a stream.
They haven't spotted that Hyaenodon is watching from nearby.
0:00
In a blur of motion, Hyaenodon rushes from its hiding place.

Digiframe™ images by Screenscene (Harrogate) Ltd.

DATA BANK 2

DOEDICURUS

(dee-dik-YOO-russ)

•SIZE: 4 metres long, 1.5 metres high – the size of a small car!
•LIVED: 2 million – 15,000 years ago
•DIET: Plants and leaves, but it probably dug in the ground for roots as well
•DID YOU KNOW: *Doedicurus* is related to modern sloths and armadillos

Some people think that they may have still been alive when humans first arrived in South America!

DATA BANK 3

DEINOTHERIUM

(dy-noh-THEER-ee-um)

- SIZE: Up to 4 metres high
- LIVED: 20 – 1.5 million years ago
- DIET: Leaves and bark from trees

- DID YOU KNOW: *Deinotherium* probably used its tusks to strip bark from trees

THE STORY OF THE

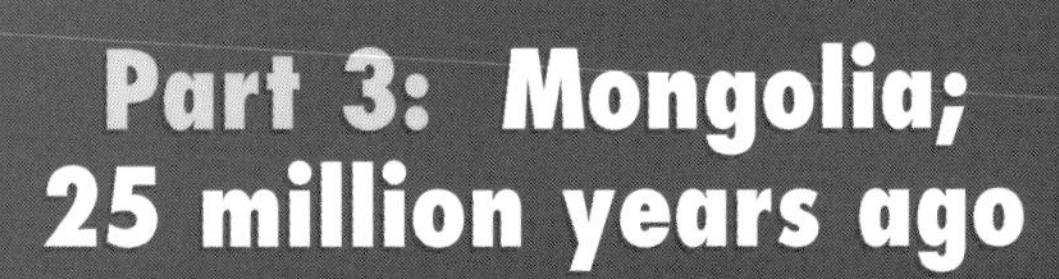

On the Mongolian plains, *Hyaenodon* are the most successful predators. Hunting in packs, they are a force to be reckoned with.

But even after doing all the hard work of catching its food, a top predator can never relax...

Because in the land of the beasts, there is always something bigger and badder than you just around the corner...

BEASTS

Part 4: Ethiopia; 3 million years ago

Grass is now firmly established and the Ethiopian plains support a wide variety of grazers and browsers.

Among them is one of the biggest beasts ever – *Deinotherium*. At 4 metres high it is a truly breath-taking beast.

But living amid the trees is another remarkable species – *Australopithecus*. A type of ape that walks on two legs, they are our very earliest ancestors!

graze/browse: nibble plants

TOP CAT

***Smilodon*, the sabre-tooth killer, was certainly no pussycat. Here's a look at what those teeth are all about:**

Sabre-tooth cats had to be careful biting an animal while it was moving. They might have broken their teeth – which were the size of carving knives!

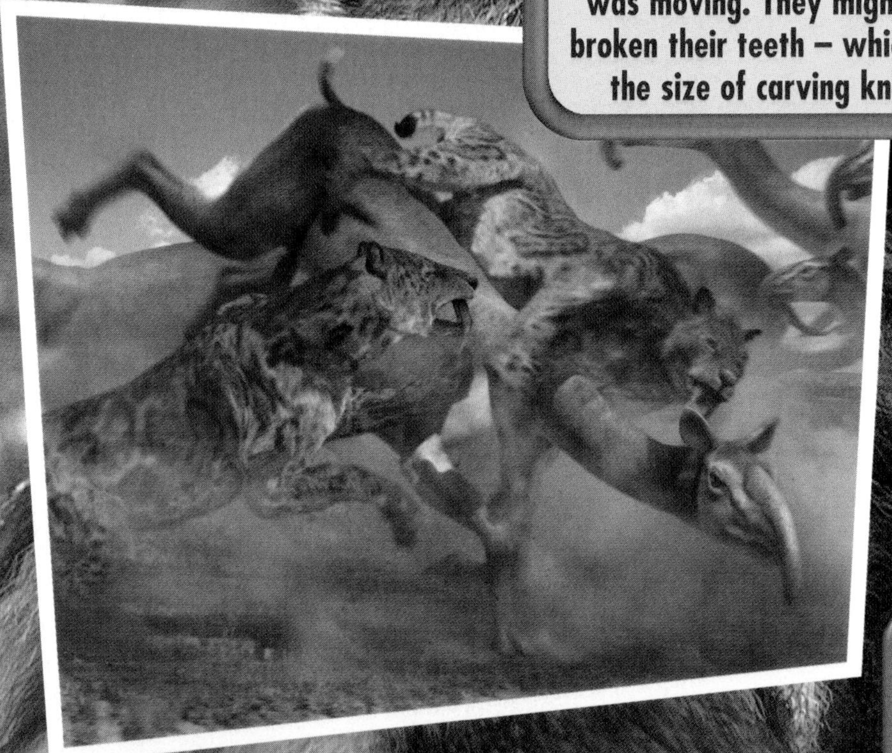

Some animals were out of even *Smilodon's* league. At up to 6 metres in length and with claws up to 30cm long, *Megatherium* feared nothing.

Smilodon wasn't a very efficient hunter. It could only eat the fleshier parts of its prey and left most of it uneaten – so they had to hunt more often. They hunted a lot in forests – it was much easier to sneak up on other beasts there.
SMILODON
(SMY-loh-don)
FULL NAME: *Smilodon populator*
MEANS: 'Knife tooth'
WHEN: 1.5 – 0.1 million years ago
WHERE: Fossils have been found in North and South America (Brazil, Argentina and Bolivia)
SIZE: Up to 1.2 metres high

PICT
TH

It's not an easy task to bring such startling beasts to life on our television screens – it took 18 months of hard work to finish all the computer effects! Here's how the team used some movie magic to take us back in time – we hope you think all the hard work was worth it.

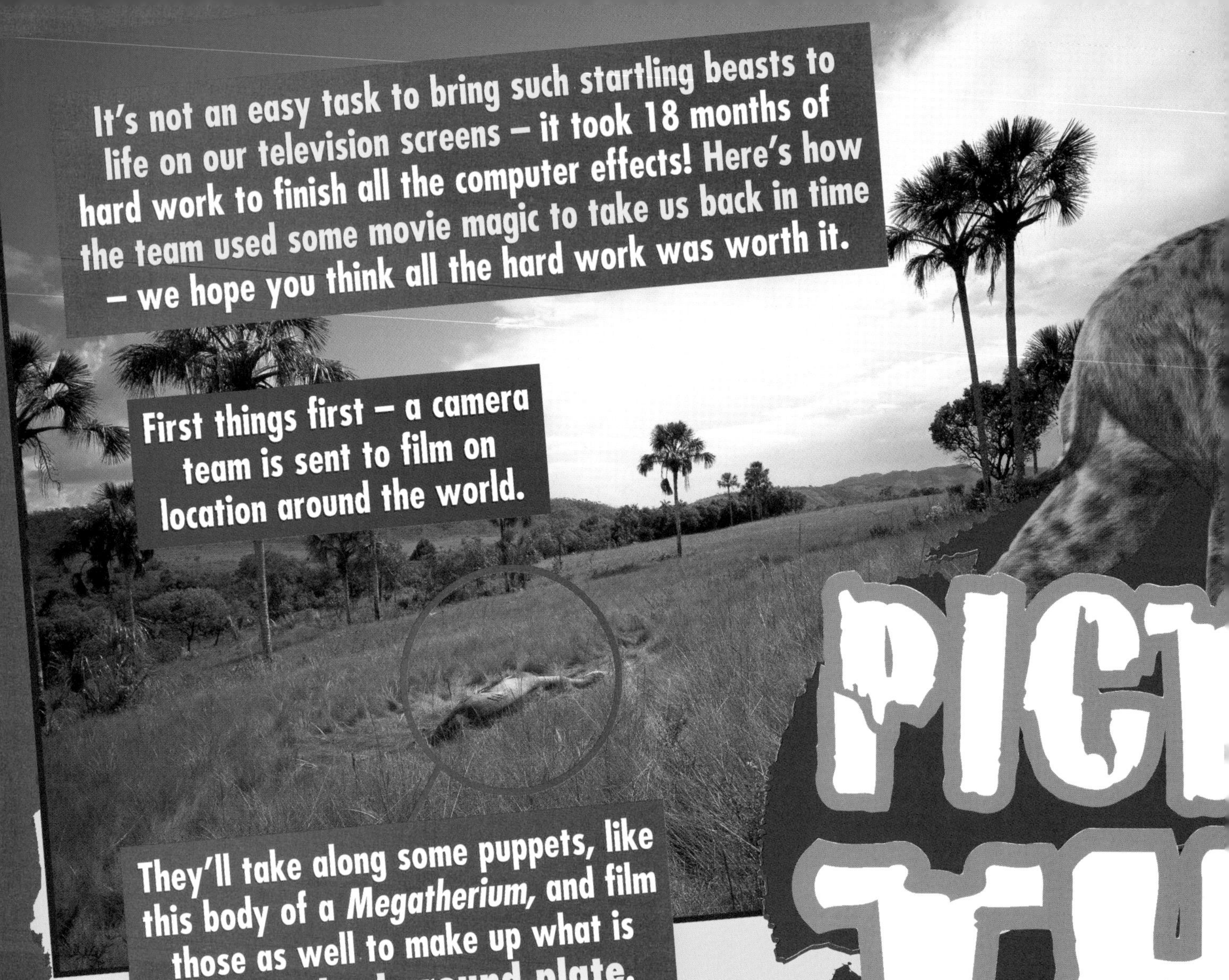

First things first – a camera team is sent to film on location around the world.

They'll take along some puppets, like this body of a *Megatherium,* and film those as well to make up what is called the **background plate.**

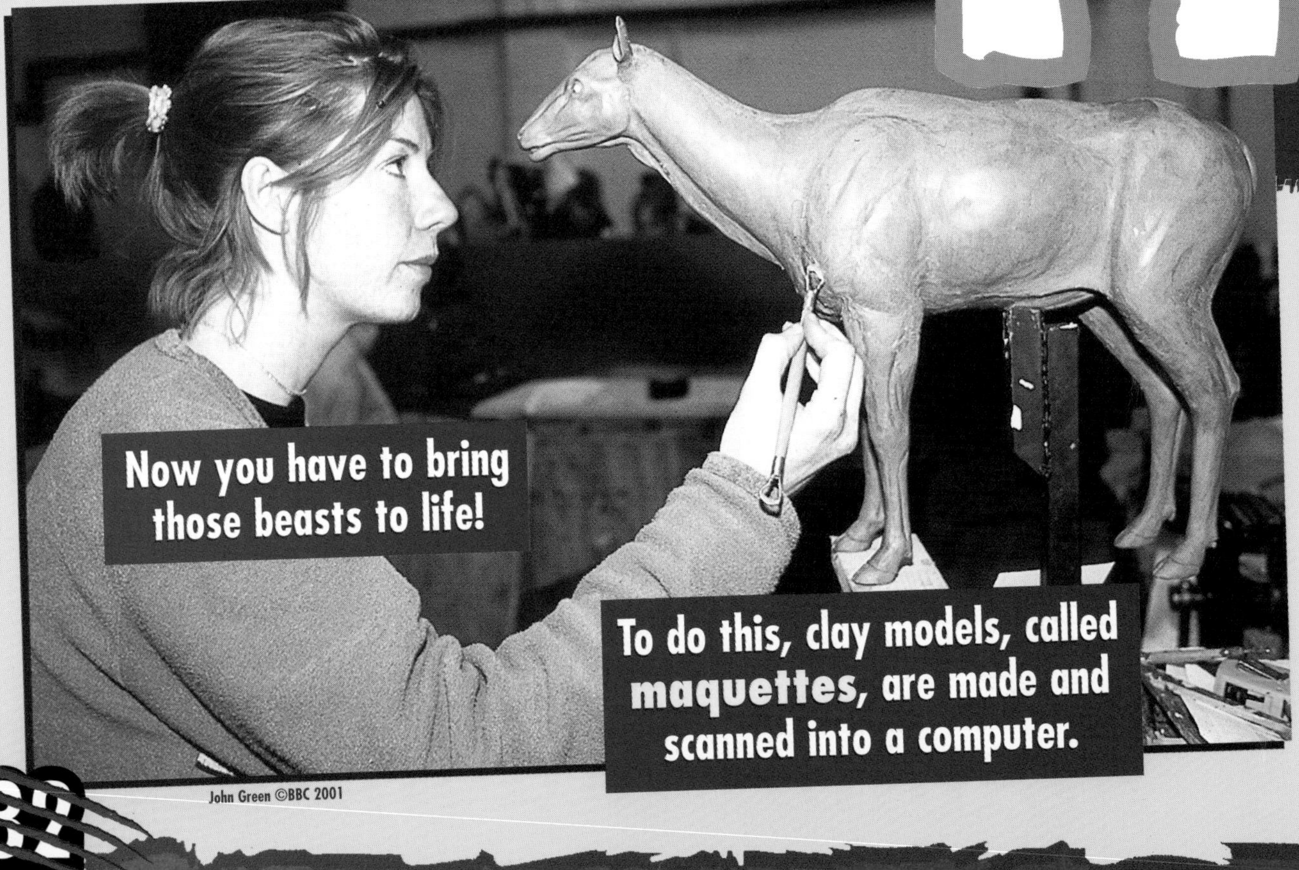

Now you have to bring those beasts to life!

To do this, clay models, called **maquettes**, are made and scanned into a computer.

John Green ©BBC 2001

URE

IS

Detail is then added by computer artists to make a final **digital** model of each beast.

The digital beasts are then added to the original background plate. This is called **compositing**.

Extra dust clouds and other effects are also added to make it look like the beasts were really there.

This has to be done for every frame of film, and there are 25 of those for each second you see on television – phew!

LIGHTS, CAMERA, ACTION!

Play this board game with friends, and see who gets their programme made first! Take turns to roll a dice and move around the board. First one to the end wins! Good luck!

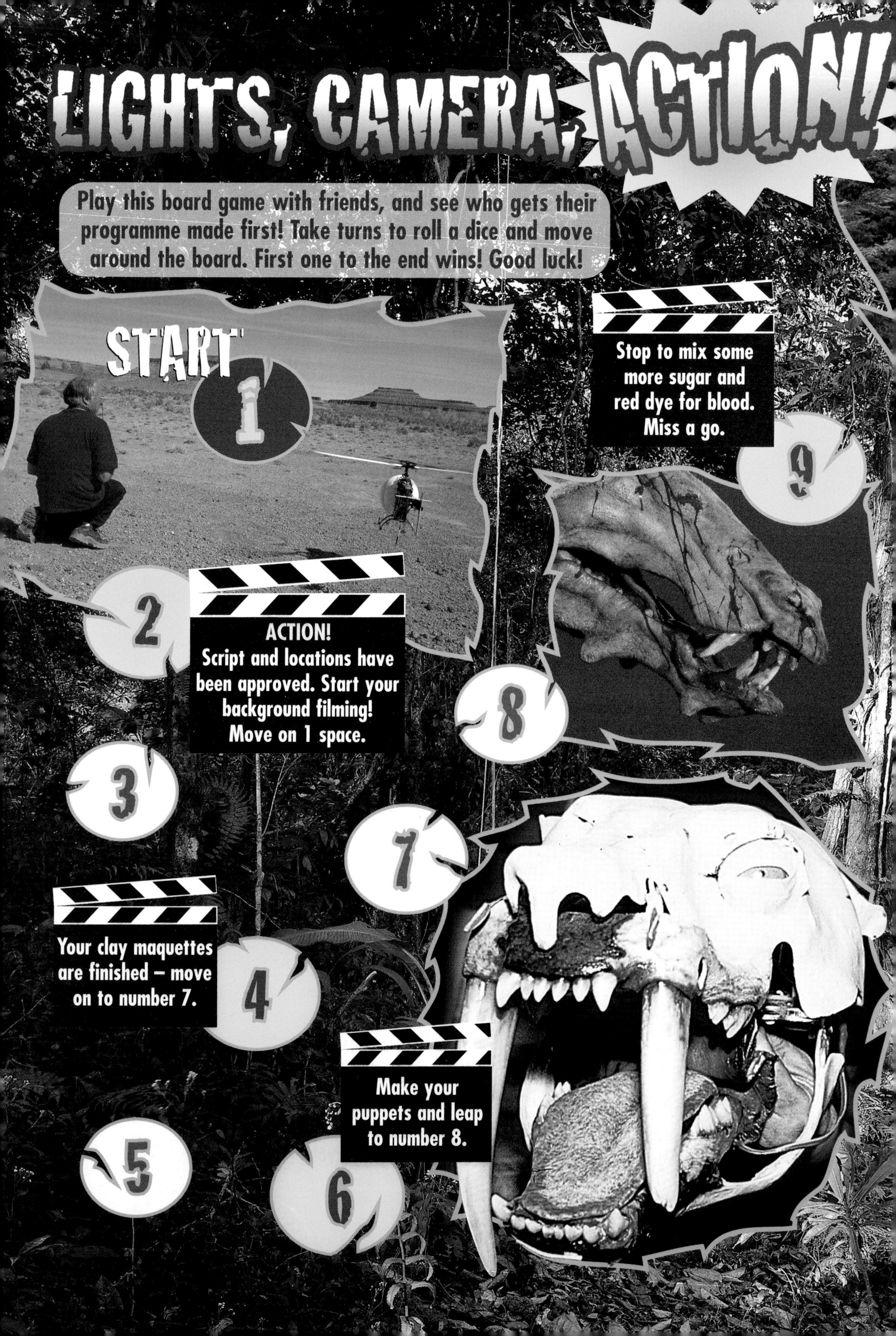

11
12
TAKE 5!
There's a problem with the *Mammoth*. Go back to 11 to sort it out.
13
14
10
KEEP ROLLING!
Filming is taking time. Roll a 6 to move again.
KEEP ROLLING!
It's going well. Roll again!
15
Well done! You're the winner.
20
16
ON AIR!
WALKING WITH BEASTS
19
CUT!
Time to edit all the material. Miss a go.
17
18

YOU DON'T SAY!
Here are some things that we found out about the beasts, proving that they don't just look very strange...
Mammoths had small ears to prevent them from losing heat in the fierce Ice Age winters.
Ambulocetus didn't have ears!
Propalaeotherium is one of the earliest types of horse.
One group of early humans seems to have specialised in hunting tortoises!

Female *Smilodons* took no part in any hunts, they were too busy protecting their young.
Chalicothere had such long claws on its front legs that it couldn't put them flat on the ground. So it had to walk on its knuckles!
Macrauchenia was originally discovered by Charles Darwin, who famously suggested that humans were related to apes.
Formicium was a type of ant up to 3cm long that ate other animals!
Hunting in packs, especially at night, *Hyaenodon* were like the lions of their times, prowling the plains.

WORK IT OUT

We've mixed up three beasts. Can you work out which bits belong to which beast? Write the letters in the boxes, with the name of beast in the spaces below.

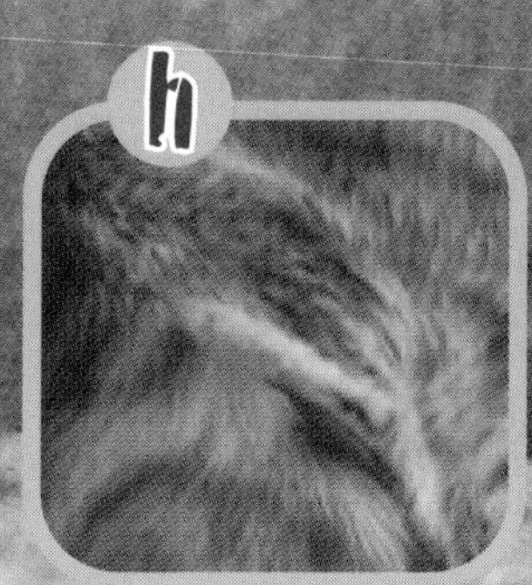

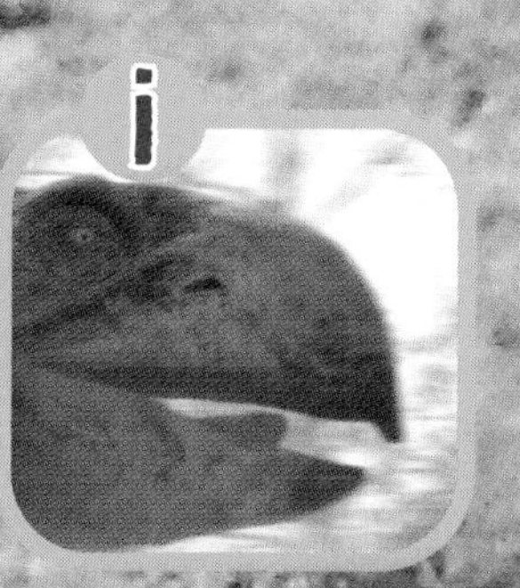

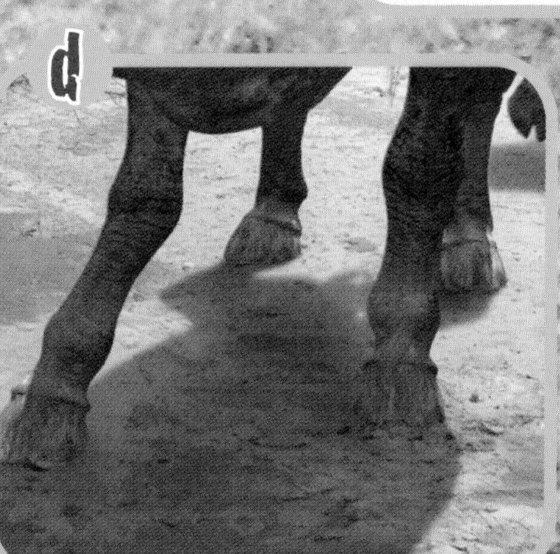

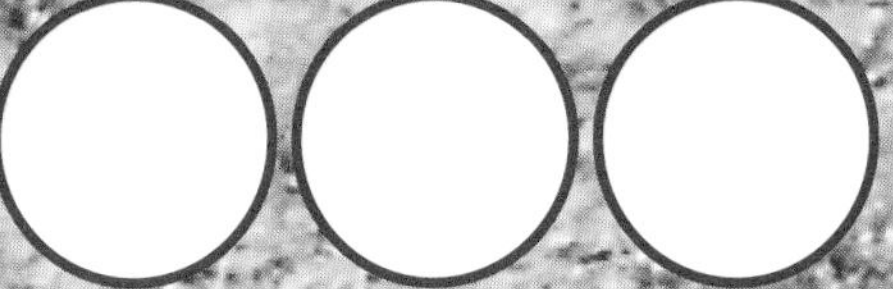

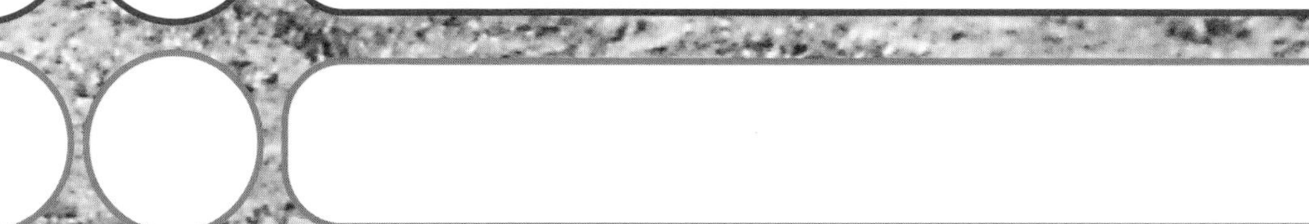

Circle the four differences between these pictures of two Indricotheres drinking.

Answers:

a,d,e is Entelodont, b,g,h is *Smilodon* c,f,i is *Gastornis*

Spot the difference: A leg and the tail on the left Indricothere have vanished, a bird above the right Indricothere has gone, the two birds in the water have disappeared.

JUMBO GIANT

Meet a monster *Mammoth* and find out more about this Ice Age giant...

***Mammoths* lived in an Ice Age which tested even the most magnificent of beasts. Fresh snow often hid thin layers of ice, which became dangerous traps for these creatures.**

They were herbivorous, eating only grass and twigs – up to 180kg of grass a day. That's about as heavy as 2 grown-ups or 2800 bars of chocolate!

MAMMOTH (MAM-oth)

FULL NAME: *Mammuthus primigenius*

MEANS: 'Earth mole'

WHEN: 135,000 – 11,000 years ago

WHERE: Fossils have been found in Ireland, eastern North America and Siberia

SIZE: Up to 3 metres tall – almost as tall as a house!

WHAT HAPPENED NEXT?

We know that these amazing beasts are no longer around, but could any animals today be a distant cousin? Read on to find out more – you may be surprised!

This small burrowing mammal is an armadillo and is related to *Doedicurus*. Both are covered with strong bony plates for protection.

Chalicothere would have walked on its knuckles because of its long, curved claws – like the way a gorilla walks.

Chalicotheres are divided into two different groups. One lived in open areas and browsed like goats, but the other lived in woodland and was more like a modern gorilla.

Animal photography: Bruce Coleman collection.

PREHISTORIC PUZZLES

Look carefully at these pictures of *Megaloceros* and then circle the odd one out.

Read the clues and write your answer in the space below.

WHO AM I?

I'm able to walk on land,
Although water is a halfway house.
I catch my prey by drowning them,
I'm not a cat or mouse.

Need one more clue?

My family will become the greatest mammals of all time – the whales.

Andrewsarchus has gobbled some letters out of these names. Replace the missing letters to complete the names.

c r n e P u o l y h g M

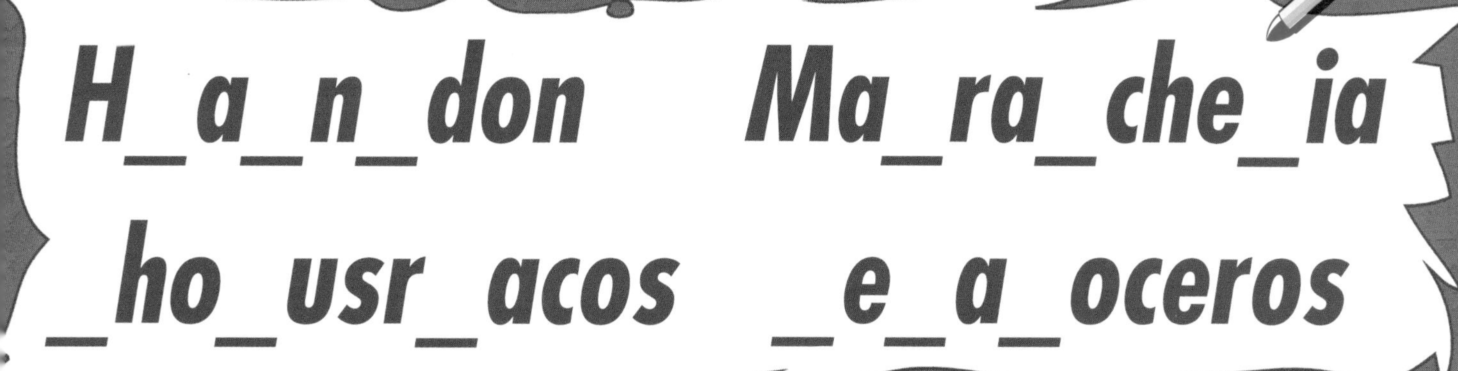

TRUE OR FALSE?

1) *Mammoths* kept warm by flapping their big ears.

2) The armadillo is a distant relative of *Doedicurus.*

3) *Godinotia* was scared of the dark.

4) *Megatherium* was up to 6 metres long.

Answers:

The beast names are: *Hyaenodon*, *Macrauchenia*, *Phorusrhacos* and *Megaloceros*. 1) false, 2) true, 3) false, 4) true.

Picture c is the odd one out. The mystery beast is *Ambulocetus*.

THE STORY OF THE

Part 5: Paraguay; 1.6 million years ago

South America has been separate from the rest of the world for 30 million years, and the beasts here are like nothing else on the planet.

With its Terror Birds and huge, armoured herbivores, it is a land of strange giants.

But recently 2 continents collided. Now there is a clear path to North America – and there's a new predator in town...

continent: large mass of land e.g. Europe

BEASTS

Part 6: Northern Europe; 30,000 years ago

A bitter Ice Age winter is around the corner, but now is a time of plenty.

Bison, horses and reindeer graze the plains in their millions. With so many beasts gathering, the predators have also come.

In the long history of the world, there have been few hunters more skilled than this...

...the direct ancestor of modern man.

WALKING WITH

KEY:
a: *Moeritherium*
b: *Macrauchenia*
c: *Phorusrhacos*
d: *Smilodon*
e: *Megaloceros*
f: Indricothere
g: *Godinotia*
h: *Chalicothere*
i: *Mammoth*

c

f

b

e

a

d

Thanks to Miles. Child photography by Christopher Baines.

THE BEASTS

Part 2

Here's another chance to put some more of these massive beasts into perspective:

COPY AND DRAW

TOP TIP:
Start in the middle and work your way out, copying one square at a time.

TOP TIP:
Add a white line to the tooth to make it look really sharp.

Use the grid below to help you copy the other sides of these pictures and finish them off.

TOP TIP:
Don't try to do too much at once – start by drawing the outline and then fill in the details.

TOP TIP:
Use thin pencil marks for the whiskers.

So how much do you know about the prehistoric world of beasts? Test your know-how with our monster quiz. Write your answers on a piece of paper!

LEVEL 1: BEASTS BASICS

1. Which beast is this?
2. What sort of things did *Godinotia* eat?
3. Which beast had small ears to prevent it losing heat in the Ice Age winters?
4. How do you say *Chalicothere*?
   a) KAL-ik-oh-theer
   b) CHAL-ik-OH-theer
5. Could *Ambulocetus* swim?
6. Which is bigger, *Leptictidium* or Entelodont?
7. Whose name means 'King Lizard'?
8. How long ago did *Dorudon* live?
9. True or False? *Hyaenodon* has spots on its back.
10. What type of beast was *Formicium*?
11. What does 'Smilodon' mean?
12. What did *Mammoths* eat?

13 True or false? *Female Smilodons* did all the fighting.

14 Which two beasts did you learn to draw on pages 18-19?

15 True or False? *Godinotia* was a small pig.

16 Which beast had claws up to 30cm long?

17 True or False? *Basilosaurus* only ate things that lived in the sea.

18 Which one of these beasts is a meat-eater: Brontothere or *Dinofelis*?

19 True or false? *Walking with Beasts* is the follow-up to *Walking with Dinosaurs.*

20 Which beast is on the cover of the annual – no peeking!

21 Where did *Megaloceros* live?

22 How many legs does *Moeritherium* have?

23 True or False? *Mammoth* fossils have been found in Ireland.

24 True or False? *Chalicothere* walked on its knuckles because its legs were too short.

25 Which beast gobbled the letters on page 45?

Answers:

1) *Gastornis*
2) Mainly insects, but also fruit
3) *Mammoth*
4) a: KAL-ik-oh-theer
5) Yes, it could
6) Entelodont
7) *Basilosaurus*
8) 40-36 million years ago
9) False
10) An ant
11) Knife tooth
12) Grass and twigs
13) False
14) *Phorusrhacos* and *Doedicurus*
15) False
16) *Megatherium*
17) False
18) *Dinofelis*
19) True
20) *Smilodon*
21) All over Europe
22) Four
23) True
24) False – it walked on its knuckles because its claws were so long
25) *Andrewsarchus*

How did you score?

0-5: Oh dear! Head back to page 1 and see if you can do better next time.
6-10: Ooops, better try again or you'll be next on a *Smilodon's* menu!
11-15: You might last a few days in the world of beasts, but you need to brush up on your survival skills.
16-20: You certainly know your *Megaloceros* from your *Megatherium*, but there's room for improvement.
21-4: So you know your basics. Now try for the expert level...
25: That was too easy! Turn over for a real test...

So you've covered the basics, but are you a real Beast Master? Try these questions and see if you can make the grade...

LEVEL 2: EXPERT

1. How much grass did a *Mammoth* eat on average per day?
2. How did *Andrewsarchus* get its name?
3. Which beast was the earliest type of horse?
4. Where did *Leptictidium* live?
5. Who originally discovered *Macrauchenia* – Charles Darwin or Tim Haines?
6. Where was Episode 5 filmed?
7. Which creature was a sleep-swimmer?
8. Why did people think *Megaloceros* died out?
9. True or false? *Ambulocetus* had no ears.
10. What are the two main living relatives of *Doedicurus*?
11. True or False? *Andrewsarchus* ate turtles.
12. How many frames are there in every second of film?
13. What is the proper name given to the clay models that are made of the beasts?
14. What is the proper name for the process of adding the computer images of beasts to the background film?

15 True or False? *Deinotherium* was one of the beasts to find in Mammoth mission on pages 10-11.

16 Which one weighs more – an elephant or Indricothere?

17 When did *Hyaenodon* prefer to hunt – during the day or during the night?

18 Which beast lived longest ago – Indricothere or *Leptictidium*?

19 Up to how many people were needed to work the full-size *Mammoth* puppet?

20 How long did it take to finish all the computer effects?

21 What was the fake blood made from?

22 True or false? *Walking with Beasts* was filmed in Bournemouth.

23 Where in Egypt would you find remains of *Moeritherium*?

24 Which beast probably used its tusks to strip bark from trees?

25 How many scientists were involved in the making of the series?

Bonus Beast Master Question: What is the modern full name of Indricothere? Now spell it!

Answers:

1) 180kg
2) It is named after the palaeontologist, Roy Chapman Andrews
3) *Propalaeotherium*
4) Tropical forests in Kazakstan
5) Charles Darwin
6) Brazil
7) *Basilosaurus*
8) Because its horns were too large!
9) True
10) Sloth and armadillo
11) True
12) 25
13) Maquettes
14) Compositing
15) False
16) Indricothere
17) During the night
18) *Leptictidium*
19) Seven
20) 18 months
21) Sugar syrup and red dye
22) False
23) Fayum deposits
24) *Deinotherium*
25) At least 400!

Bonus: *Paraceratherium transouralicum*

How did you score?

0-5: Looks like 'Beast Master' was just a step too far...

6-10: You might manage to dodge *Doedicurus* but *Gastornis* would still get you!

11-15: You're certainly no *Neanderthal*, but there's still a way to go...

16-20: Ooops, you slipped up on the thin ice, but you're on the right track.

21-4: What an expert! Are you sure you've never done this before?

25: Whoa! Move over Tim Haines, there's a new guy in town!

25 + the bonus question: You really are the 'Beast Master'! So when is *your* series coming out?

FOLLOWING UP

There is more information about these beasts out there than you may think:

A good place to start is your local museum

Or you could try the Natural History Museum in London (www.nhm.ac.uk)

You can also check out the *Walking with Beasts* website at: www.bbc.co.uk/beasts

And remember the programme is on BBC 1!

Here are the answers to Mammoth mission:

L	E	P	T	I	C	T	I	D	I	U	M
A	U	H	T	N	O	D	O	L	I	M	S
N	E	O	G	C	B	A	S	X	U	E	U
C	A	R	E	K	A	V	A	I	A	G	C
Y	O	U	S	H	S	A	R	A	A	A	E
L	A	S	T	A	T	E	A	I	N	T	H
O	T	R	H	T	O	M	M	A	M	H	T
T	U	H	R	T	A	S	L	S	A	E	I
H	Q	A	O	A	L	A	I	Y	N	R	P
E	L	C	I	O	K	N	U	A	C	I	O
R	A	O	S	A	R	S	A	P	A	U	L
I	C	S	A	O	T	O	L	Y	C	M	A
U	N	C	T	L	O	T	H	E	R	I	R
M	E	S	A	J	R	A	G	T	B	A	T
A	A	D	O	E	D	I	C	U	R	U	S
G	A	S	A	T	A	P	L	J	K	E	U
A	M	B	U	L	O	C	E	T	U	S	A

To make your **LITTLE BOOK OF BIG BEASTS**

1 Carefully cut along the white dotted lines.

2 Fold the pages down the centre, making sure the cover is on the outside.

3 Now just put the other pages inside, with the numbers in the correct order, and your book is ready!

7 ANDREWSARCHUS

FULL NAME: *Andrewsarchus mongoliensis* (and-rooz-ARK-uss)

MEANS: 'Andrew's beast.' It is named after Roy Chapman Andrews – the role model for Indiana Jones!

WHEN: 60 – 32 million years ago

WHERE: Mongolia

SIZE: About 1.8 metres high and 5 metres long, with a skull nearly a metre long! It was the largest meat eating land mammal ever.

DIET: Meat, maybe using their huge jaws to crush turtles and catch crocodiles

LITTLE BOOK OF BIG BEASTS

WALKING WITH BEASTS

1 ENTELODONT

FULL NAME: *Parahyus orientalis*

MEANS: Entelodont (en-TELL-oh-dont) means 'Perfect toothed'

WHEN: 45 – 25 million years ago

WHERE: Mongolia

SIZE: 2.1 metres high at the shoulder. That's taller than most grown-ups!

DIET: Mainly scavenged meat from other beast's kills, but would eat anything!

6 MEGATHERIUM

FULL NAME: *Megatherium americanum* (meg-ah-THEER-ee-um)

WHERE: South America – north as far as Texas and as far south as Argentina

MEANS: 'Giant beast'

WHEN: 1.9 million – 8,000 years ago

SIZE: Up to 6 metres long, it weighed almost 4 tonnes. That's about the same as an elephant

DIET: Mainly browsed on vegetation, but it may have eaten the meat from other dead animals, too

5 GASTORNIS

FULL NAME: *Gastornis geiselensis* (gas-TOR-niss)

MEANS: 'Gaston's bird.' Named after Gaston Planté, who found the first remains

WHEN: 56 – 41 million years ago

WHERE: Remains have been found in Germany and America

SIZE: 1.75 metres tall

DIET: The meat of anything too slow to escape!

2 CHALICOTHERE

FULL NAME: *Chalicothere* (KAL-ik-oh-theer) is based on *Chalicotherium*

MEANS: 'Pebble beast'

WHEN: 45 – 3.5 million years ago

WHERE: Remains have been found in Europe and Asia

SIZE: Males were up to 2.6 metres tall, and females up to 1.8 metres.

DIET: It only ate soft shoots from trees

3 INDRICOTHERE

FULL NAME: *Paraceratherium transouralicum* (but it used to be called *Indricotherium*)

MEANS: 'Indrik beast.' The indrik was a fairy-tale Russian beast like a unicorn.

WHEN: 30 – 25 million years ago

WHERE: Mongolia

SIZE: Around 4.5 metres tall and weighed over 15 tonnes!

DIET: They browsed on the leaves from the top of trees – a bit like modern giraffes.

4 DINOFELIS

FULL NAME: *Dinofelis barlowi* (dy-noh-FEE-liss)

MEANS: 'Terrible cat'

WHEN: 5 – 1.4 million years ago

WHERE: Africa, North America, Asia and Europe

SIZE: 0.7 metres high at the shoulder

DIET: Meat – especially baboons and *Australopithecus*